THE MYSTERIOUS ADVENTURES OF CAVE EXPRESS

By: Steven Jestes
Illustrated By: Robert Florio

Volume I

Introduction:
Water all around me
There is no sky
26 years ago, I used to be alive

I used to be alive...

I woke up knowing today was going to be the best day of my life. My name is Katie and my twin brother's name is Thomas. We are traveling to visit our grandmother. It takes three hours by boat to arrive at her house. Her house is in the middle of the water off the Gulf coast. How cool is that?! The reason Thomas and I like to visit our grandmother is because she always has these great adventures for us to go on. She always has interesting stories to tell and she ALWAYS has the best lemonade.

Thomas had trouble getting ready on time. Mom said we were going to leave at 6:00 a.m. but Thomas made us 15 minutes late. My mother was talking to my father on the phone and I heard her say, "Thomas made us leave a quarter after six." I asked her on the boat ride and she said, "15 minutes after 6 or 6:15 is called a quarter after 6 and if we left at 5:45 it would be a quarter till 6." I sighed and said, "I'll never learn anything." Mom laughed and said, "The older you get the more you'll understand." I don't know why she always says that. There are so many things I don't understand, and I have this fear that I will never learn anything. I get this feeling a lot during the school year. Whenever I am swamped with schoolwork, I want to give up because I don't think I will be able to make it. Sure enough, I get through the school year just fine.

It was sunny on our boat ride to Grandmother's house. My mom packed me a roast beef sandwich with lettuce, and she made Thomas a baloney sandwich. That's all Thomas eats - baloney, baloney, and more baloney. I like to eat roast beef, turkey, ham, and I love hamburgers. My mom makes us eat healthy so we don't get to put any mayonnaise on our sandwiches. She also makes us drink water. That is why I like to go to Grandma's, because she makes us lemonade.

The bay is beautiful; it looks like thousands of diamonds spread out across the water as the sun comes up. I am really starting to get anxious. I cannot wait to get to Grandma's house. Thomas and I get to see her once a year right before school starts. My mom said that she is starting to get sick and she wants us to see her more. I asked my mom if we could stay there for the whole year, but she did not like the idea. Thomas and I start the sixth grade and a new school in 3 weeks. The summer is almost over. I don't like the idea of summer being over just like my mom doesn't like the idea of me staying with Grandma for a year.

We are about 30 minutes away from Grandma's house. We can see some of the houses on the shore as we travel by on boat. Every time we pass this house painted bright green, I know we are 30 minutes away. Thomas used to ask if we can paint our house bright green and my mom would laugh and said no. Thomas's favorite color is green. One time my mom found him in the bathroom coloring his arms and face green with a Magic Marker. Now that he is older, the story embarrasses him. I like to tease him about it every occasionally. He gets upset, but he doesn't mind too much.

Tomorrow the weatherman is calling for heavy rain. I really hope it does rain. My grandmother and grandfather were both award-winning architects. When my grandfather was in his 30's, the Queen of England selected him to design a summer home in the United States. I never got a chance to meet my grandfather; he passed away before Thomas and I were born. After my grandfather and grandmother retired, they spent 3 years building this amazing house in the middle of the water. I like the roof the best. It has all these different sized tubes and some of them travel through the house. Whenever it rains, each tube collects water and you hear this amazing chiming noise that sounds like you are in the rain forest. It is like nothing you have ever heard or seen before. About two feet below the ceiling, there are shelves with flowers flowing around the entire room. They sit in individual pots and they are organized by color. The family room has green flowers, the kitchen has yellow flowers, Grandma's bedroom has red flowers, the hallways have white flowers, and the guest bedroom Thomas and I sleep in has blue flowers. One of the tubes from the roof flows across the entire ceiling of the house slightly above the flowers. When it rains, the tube waters the flowers. There are tiny holes at the bottom of the tube and rainwater drips into the flowers making a unique dripping sound. Some of the tubes go through the house and you can see the water travel through them. There is one room in the house Thomas and I have not seen before. We were never allowed to go into it. All of the tubes in the house connect to this room, too! Grandmother says the room is magical. She said that when we were old enough to make reasonable decisions we could explore the room. I never knew what she meant by that, but every time we visit Thomas and I always beg Grandma to let us in the room.

Thomas: "We're here! We're here!"

Mom parked the boat at the dock next to the house, and Thomas and I ran up to hug Grandma. Grandma always cries every time we see her because she is so excited to see us. She told us to go in and pour ourselves a glass of lemonade while she talked to my mom outside. Finally, Thomas and I get to drink something other then water. As I walked into the house, I noticed that the flowers were missing. Instead of flowers, she had tiny bonsai trees. Now the house really looks like a rainforest. The last time we visited, Thomas and I helped her put all of the yellow flowers in the kitchen. Next to the house, she has two paddleboats that she uses to travel to her garden. She and Grandpa made a small island about 40 feet away from the house. She grows lemons, tomatoes, apples, flowers, beans, potatoes, and all sorts of things out there. She only travels to the store twice a month and she uses the garden to make all of her food. She doesn't like to get out much; she enjoys staying at home.

Grandmother: "I hope you kids are ready for an adventure. They are calling for a big rain storm tomorrow, and I have decided to let you explore the secret room."

Thomas: "Really Grandma! Are we old enough now?"

Grandmother: "Yes, your mother and I have been talking about this for the last month, and we feel you are old enough. Remember, the choices you make in the room will stay with you for the rest of your life. You must think before you act on any decision. Whether you know it or not, each decision you make in life will determine your future."

Katie: "What if we make a wrong decision Grandma?"

Grandmother: "I trust you both to make the right decisions. You are both very smart. If you have a hard time figuring something out, just stop and think about the consequences of your actions. I promise if you do this, you will be on the path to making all the right decisions in life."

Thomas: "Grandma, what is in the room? Why do the tubes from the roof travel into the room?"

Grandmother: "You must be patient. You will just have to wait until tomorrow morning."

After Grandma told Thomas that he would have to wait until tomorrow morning, he paused for a moment with a smile on his face. Then he ran into the kitchen for more lemonade. I told him to pour me a glass, too. We sat at the kitchen table and looked out at the ocean. You can

see the garden from a distance. Grandma said that we
would be leaving to go to the garden on the paddleboats
in about an hour to pick some strawberries for dinner.
Strawberries are my favorite fruit in the world. Thomas
and Grandma like them a lot, too. If I could, I would eat
them all day.

After Thomas and I finished our glass of
lemonade, we went into the guest room to make our beds.
We also put everything we had packed from home in the
room. After we finished doing this, it was time for
Grandma to take us to the garden. We walked outside and
Grandma untied the paddleboats from the dock. I rode
with Grandma, and Thomas got his own paddleboat. I like
being with Grandma. She always has a smile on her face.
She loves to tell stories about mother when she was
younger. Thomas and I like those the best. Everything
she says is so interesting.

Thomas raced to the garden and got there before
us. As Grandma and I reached the garden, we tied both
of the boats to the dock so they would not float away. In
the garden, there are many rows where you can walk to
get to each tree or plant. Grandma gave both Thomas and
me a bucket and said to run all the way to the end and
make a right. That is where all the strawberries are.
Thomas said he was going to pick more strawberries then
I was, and I told him it was fine because I was going to
eat them all anyway. Grandma finally made it over to help
us pick strawberries.

Grandmother: "Would you all like to hear how Grandpa

and I built this small island?"

Katie: "Yes!"

Thomas: "Sure Grandma."

Grandmother: "After your grandfather and I retired, we spent 3 years building the house over there. We had been planning and designing for over 5 years in our spare time. While we were building the main house, Grandpa would spend an hour a day going to Uncle Bill's plastic factory. He had all sorts of things like plastic bottles and plastic silverware. Every time he visited the plastic factory, he would make medium-sized plastic balls that could float. Each visit he would make about 100 plastic balls. After 3 years, he made 109,500 plastic balls used to make the island float. He then made a net out of rope to hold 100 balls at one time. He made 1,095 nets; each filled with 100 plastic balls and built a foundation of bamboo and plywood over top of the plastic nets. Each net is connected to the foundation so you don't have to worry about the island sinking. After he built the foundation, he added dirt and sand to the top and planted many different trees and plants all around. Even though it was a lot of work, your grandfather and I loved to build and design things. It was our greatest hobby. We built the garden so we would not have to travel to the store. Everything I need to live on is right here. Your grandfather spent about 2 hours each day building the island, and after 2 years, it was finally complete. If you dedicate a little bit of time each day to something you really want, your dreams will come true.

Katie: "Thomas and I spend a half hour each day building a Lego house. Mom made us build one for a summer project. She said if we finish it, she would take us to any amusement park we want."

Grandmother: "That is excellent, guys; your mother is already teaching you life lessons that will get you very far."

Thomas: "But Grandma, why wouldn't you want to go to the store?"

Grandmother: "Because when you get old, you can't get out as much as you did before. I can't do the things I used to be able to do when I was young."

Katie: "Grandma, I don't want you to get old. I want you to live forever."

Grandmother: "You are so sweet Katie; you truly are. However, we all grow old. It is the natural way of life. There are things in life we may not like, but we have to accept them for what they are. On a brighter note, I think we have enough strawberries. How about if we go back, and I'll make us some dinner while you two cut up the strawberries?"

Thomas: "Yeah, let's do that. I'm starving!"

Thomas got back into his paddleboat and made it back before Grandma and me again. We went inside and Thomas and I started washing the strawberries and cutting off the stems. After we prepared the strawberries, we placed them in another bucket for dinner. Grandmother was making tomato soup and grilled cheese sandwiches. Thomas and I finished washing and cutting up all of the strawberries at the same time Grandmother finished making dinner. We ate the strawberries with our meal, and Thomas and I both had another glass of lemonade.

Grandmother: "Katie, how are things going at home?"

Katie: "Things are going great. We don't get to see Dad as much as we would like though. He is always away at work. Last week, he was gone on business, and we didn't see him at all. Mom usually takes us to the pool in the afternoon when it's really hot outside. A few of my friends from school go to the pool, too."

Grandmother: "I heard you two are starting a new school in 3 weeks? Are you going to have the Lego house done in time to go to the amusement park before school starts?"

Thomas: "The Lego house is almost finished. Katie is building the rest of the deck in the back of the house, and I am finishing the roof. Then we will be done. I think we will have it completed next week. We have spent a lot of time on it."

Grandmother: "That is wonderful guys. Do you have an amusement park picked out?"

Katie: "I want to go to Disney World!"

Thomas: "Yeah, me too!"

Grandmother: "You know, your grandfather and I took your mother to Disney World when she was about your age."

Katie: "Really?! Do you want to come with us Grandma?"

Grandmother: "I don't think I will be able to make it this time children; Grandma is getting old."

Katie: "You're not getting old, Grandma. You can still paddle a boat with us to the island and pick strawberries."

Grandmother: "You are right Katie, but the island is a little closer then Disney World. How about you two help me clear off the table and after we're done, we can go start a fire in the pit by the dock."

Thomas: "That sounds awesome, Grandma! Can we make S'mores, too?"

Grandmother: "It wouldn't be a fire without S'mores, Thomas."

Thomas and I helped Grandma clear dinner off the table, and then we helped her wash the dishes. After that, Thomas and I played a game of checkers to pass the time before we went out to make the fire. We had time to play three games. Thomas won two of them. He gets competitive, and when he loses, he gets angry. I don't mind losing. Sometimes I let him win so he won't get so upset. After our game of checkers, Grandma gave us some logs to carry out to the fire. We made three trips carrying wood from the house to the fire pit. Then Grandma started the fire. It was still light outside, and Grandma told us to wait until dark to make S'mores. We sat by the fire for a half hour until it got completely dark. Thomas and I went inside to help Grandma get crackers, chocolate, and marshmallows to make the S'mores. She even had sticks we could use for the marshmallows. The fire was big now. You couldn't stand too close because it was so hot. We all started to melt our marshmallows in the fire and make our S'mores.

Grandmother: "Would you two like to hear a story about your mother when she was younger?"

Katie: "Yeah, tell us a story about Mom, Grandma."

Grandmother: "Well your grandfather and I used to live about 10 miles from here in a regular house that wasn't on the water. Your mom just started the fourth grade and she would walk to school because it was right down the street about a mile away. One day she noticed a white and black dog start to follow her to school. The dog had blue eyes and the most beautiful fur coat she had ever seen. Huskies are dogs that look like wolves. They are very friendly and loyal animals. A week went by and every day your mom walked to school the dog would follow her and make sure she got there. We called the dog her protector. One day the dog disappeared, and we never saw it again. We asked a couple of the neighbors who the dog belonged to and not one person had seen or heard of this dog. About two years later when your mother was your age, something very strange happened. On October 3, 1983, your mother woke up and the dog was sleeping on the floor next to her bed; we had no idea how the dog got in the house. When your mother tried to leave the room to get ready for school, the dog stopped her and started barking. Whenever your grandfather or I tried to enter the room that day the dog growled, letting us know he would bite if we entered. Your grandfather and I assumed the dog was protecting her from something, so we let her stay in her room all day and miss school. After school was over the dog ran down stairs out of the house, we never saw him again. We never found out who the dog was or why he did what he did. It was left as a mystery. I always wonder what would have happened if your mother had gone to school that day. I guess some things are better off left unknown."

Katie: "Wow, Grandma. Mom never told us that story."

Thomas: "What do you think the dog was protecting Mom from?"

Grandmother: "I have thought about that a lot over the years, Thomas. Grandfather and I like to think the dog was her guardian angel."

Katie: "That is the strangest story I have ever heard."

Grandmother: "The story will always be left as a mystery, but I know something that is not left as a mystery."

Katie: "What is that, Grandma?"

Grandmother: "Your and Thomas's bedtime. Now go run inside and get ready for bed while I clean this up. They are calling for heavy rain tomorrow; you might be in for quite an adventure."

Thomas and I ran back inside and got into our pajamas. We couldn't stop thinking about the story Grandma told us. On top of that, we were excited about tomorrow morning. Grandmother promised us that we could explore the secret room if it were pouring down rain. It's getting really late so Grandmother came in to say good night, and Thomas and I fell right to sleep.

I woke up at 6:00 the next morning. It was raining cats and dogs outside! Every time it rains like this, I feel like I am deep in a rainforest. Thomas was still sleeping, and I did not want to wake him. Even Grandmother was sleeping, and she always wakes up before me. I like the idea of being the only one awake. I feel a sense of independence. Nobody is there to tell me what to do. I really like this feeling so I begin to explore more of the house. The family room has a large window that looks out towards the ocean. The rain is crashing down heavily. It looks like Greek gods are throwing spears into the water. Every time it rains like this, I feel like Grandmother's house is slowly sinking into the water. The tubes that feed water to the bonsai trees are on full blast right now. The water that drains from the bottom of the bonsai trees collects into another tube. This tube goes through the family room and out of the house through a small hole called a hydroelectric socket. When water travels through the hole, it collects energy used inside of the house to power appliances in the kitchen. A regular home has sockets into which you plug a cord to get electricity. In Grandma's house, think of all the tubes as electric cords.

Grandmother wakes up and joins me in the family room.

Grandmother: "Every time it rained like this, your grandfather and I would start the day by making omelettes. Would you like to help me make them, Katie?"

18

Katie: "Yeah! Omelets are my favorite! Can we add cheese? Mom doesn't let us use cheese; she says it's not healthy."

Grandmother: "Tell you what; if you go wake your brother up for breakfast, we can use cheese and my homemade strawberry jelly on toast."

Katie: "Grandmother, can I ask you a question?"

Grandmother: "Of course sweetheart, what is it?"

Katie: "Are we going to be able to explore the secret room today? You said that if it is raining hard you would let us."

Grandmother: "We will talk about this during breakfast. Now go run and get your brother; you have a big day ahead of you."

When Grandmother said that I had a big day ahead of me, I knew she was going to let us explore the secret room. I have always imagined what the room looked like, why all of the tubes connect, where they lead, why they are there. Whatever the reason may be, I was about to find out. I walked into our bedroom, and Thomas was still asleep after everyone else is up as he always is. Last school year, he made us late ten different days because he wouldn't get out of bed on time. I know he will get up when I tell him what Grandmother told me.

Katie: "Thomas! Thomas! Get up; Grandmother is making us omelettes with cheese and strawberry jelly on toast."

Thomas: "Leave me alone Katie; I want to sleep more."

Katie: "You can't Thomas! Grandmother is going to let us explore the secret room after we finish our breakfast. It's raining cats and dogs outside! Take a look for yourself."

Thomas immediately opened his eyes and ran out of the room. He ran straight for the family room. When he looked out of the window and saw how hard it was raining, he began jumping up and down on the couch. Grandmother scolded him for jumping on the sofa and told him to come in the kitchen for breakfast.

Thomas: "Is it really true Grandma? Are we really going to be able to explore the secret room today?"

Grandmother: "I think today is the perfect day for you and Katie to explore, but before I allow you to do this, I have to tell you what the room is and what the room is not. What is behind that door is not a part of this house. Behind that door is a path to a new world, a world that you and I are not a part of. The decisions you make in that world will stay with you when you return. You are old enough to make decisions on your own, but it is important for you to think carefully before you make any decisions. There are going to be times when your mother and I cannot be there to make the right decisions for you. Behind that door, you will have independence. You are free to make any decision you would like."

Katie: "But Grandma, what happens if we make the wrong decision even though we think it's the right decision?"

Grandmother: "Deep down inside, you know what is right and wrong. If you take the time to listen to what your mind and heart tell you, you will always make the right decision. Look at the time. It's already 8:00 and you two have a lot of exploring to do!"

At that moment, I was just as scared as I was excited. I had never felt this feeling before. Grandmother went into her room to get the keys to unlock the door. In the middle of the door, there were three triangular shaped locks. Grandmother gave each of us a key. We all had to turn the key to the right at the same time in order for the door to open. Grandmother was to my right and Thomas was to my left. Thomas was so excited that I was beginning to wonder if he listened to anything Grandmother told us at breakfast. Just then, the door opened. Thomas and I looked inside, but it was too dark to see anything. Grandmother went into the kitchen to get a match. She reached up to light the top right corner of the room, and suddenly, a huge flame appeared and continued to travel deep into the room. When I looked in, I saw a medium sized path. There are shelves about two feet below the ceiling. They look just like the shelves in the house that hold bonsai trees, but instead of holding bonsai trees, they are holding a flame that lights up the entire pathway. This morning is already turning into the most exciting day of my life. The tubes that connect to the secret room run down the center of the path. There are three different tubes but only one has water flowing through it.

Grandmother: "It is very important that you walk next to the tube with water flowing through it. The flow of water will guide you along your way. Do not go down any other path. I need you both to promise me that you will only follow the tube with water flowing through it."

Katie: "I promise, Grandma!"

Thomas: "I promise too, Grandma!"

Thomas and I waved goodbye as Grandmother closed the door. Our adventure began. We walked down the path very slowly at first because we did not know what to expect. Further down the path, we came to a decision. We could follow the tube with water flowing through it down one path or we could follow the other two tubes down a separate path. Thomas and I listened to Grandma and followed the tube with water flowing through it. It took us to a lagoon-type cave. There were photographs on the wall, too. There were all these photos of the ocean and tiger sharks. There were five different photos of tiger sharks and three different photos of the ocean.

Thomas and I were surprised to see photos hanging up on the wall of a cave. It looked liked someone had been living down here a long time ago. Many of the photos had dust and cobwebs all over them. We also found some old newspapers. The date said October 3, 1983.

Katie: "Wait! That is the same date Grandmother told us about in Mom's story."

Thomas: "Yeah, it is! It's the day the dog stopped Mom from leaving the house and going to school. Read the headline. It might give us some information on why the dog was protecting her."

Katie: "Ok, let me read it. It says: "13 year old boy of Fawlkin Bay Middle School disappears in the middle of the day." It says the boy went missing during the day and when he came back, it was as if he was a completely different person. The boy suffered from poor vision and when he returned, he had perfect vision. It said that many different things indicated a change in the boy that could not be explained."

Thomas: "Hmm. I wonder if Mom was supposed to be the one to turn up missing instead of the boy."

Katie: "It could be, but it still doesn't give us any hard evidence."

Thomas: "I guess Grandmother is right; it will always be left a mystery."

Thomas and I began again to follow the tube with water
flowing through it. We reached a path that lead out of
the lagoon-like cave. Thomas and I saw a gloomy and
bright light towards the end. I now understood what
Grandmother meant when she said this is not part of our
world. Thomas and I walked into a very large glass dome
that looked about a mile long and a mile wide. On the
outside of the dome, you could see a moon and a dark
orange planet that was twice as big as the moon. There
are hundreds of stars, the biggest I had ever seen. They
brightened up the entire dome like a hot summer day.
Thomas and I continued to follow the tube with water
flowing through it. It led us to a small wooden bridge.
Below the bridge was a calm stream with giant yellow
goldfish. After the bridge, we reached a maze designed
out of tall green bushes. The tube with water flowing
through it stopped at the beginning of the maze, right in
front of a sign. Thomas started to read the sign.

"If a maze is what you crave,
Be sure you stand brave.
Travel until you reach a yellow tree.
Below the tree, you will find a key.
It will take you to a place you might not understand,
A path you normally would not have planned.
Take the path and you will see,
A chance for you to be free."

Thomas and I traveled into the maze and made two right turns and a left turn. We saw a large tree with yellow leaves, and we found a key next to another sign.

"Take this key and hold it close.
It will help you when you need it most.
Three lefts and a right,
You will see a door painted white.
Take the key and open the door,
And remember the key will unlock many more."

Thomas and I made three lefts and a right. It led us to a small white door. The door was half the size we were. Thomas opened the door and kept the key in his pocket so we wouldn't lose it. Behind the door was a small path. Because the door was so small, Thomas and I had to crawl to get through it. At the end of the path, we found two black inner tubes and two tunnels with water flowing through them just like a water park. Thomas and I love water parks. We were so excited to travel down. There were two cave holes and Thomas and I jumped down at the same time. They went around in circles and up and down. It was the best ride I had ever been on. The cave spit us out at the end into a pool of water that led us to the bigger part of the cave. Thomas and I were soaking wet. After the pool of water, we found the tube with water flowing through it again. It leads to seven different doors. The tube with water flowing through it leads to the far right door.

Thomas: "I bet you the key opens all of these doors, Katie."

Katie: "We have to listen to Grandmother, Thomas. We have to follow the tube with water flowing through it."

Thomas: "No we don't. I have a key that can take me anywhere I want to go. Grandmother isn't here to tell us what to do."

Katie: "Can we just take the door with water flowing through it? I'm scared."

Thomas: "I have the key now. You have to do what I want to do, and I want to take the middle door."

Katie: "Didn't you listen to anything Grandmother said? She made us promise to follow the tube with water flowing through it."

Thomas: "Just because we promised Grandma that we would follow the tube with water flowing through it doesn't mean we have to listen to her. She will never find out. I bet you behind the middle door is something far more exciting. I'm going through the door; if you don't follow me I'm going to leave you here."

Katie: "Fine, Thomas. But if something happens to us, it's going to be your fault!"

Thomas: "Nothing is going to happen. Let's have a real adventure."

Thomas opened the middle door, and I followed him in. Beyond the door was another cave. This cave was much larger then the one before. It looked like the end went on for miles. Just then, the cave started to shake, and we could see dust and small rocks falling from the top. Thomas and I got scared because we thought the cave might collapse. We did not know what to do, so we ran back to the door for safety. All of the sudden there was a huge light coming from a distance. It sounded like a train. Thomas and I realized it actually was a train when we heard a loud horn and thick smoke coming out of it. The train slammed on its breaks and continued to slow down until it reached us. It looked like a train from the 1800's. The train finally screeched to a stop, and Thomas and I were as excited as ever to see what was inside and where the train was going.

Train Conductor: "All Aboard!"

Thomas and I entered the train, and we could not believe how fancy the inside looked. It had booths like a restaurant with red leather and solid gold tables. The ceiling was solid gold as well. Over every booth, a slightly dim light lit the cabin to create an eerie atmosphere. Thomas and I were both just as scared as we were excited. Just then, a very attractive woman with a fancy black dress walked in and told us to follow her. She took

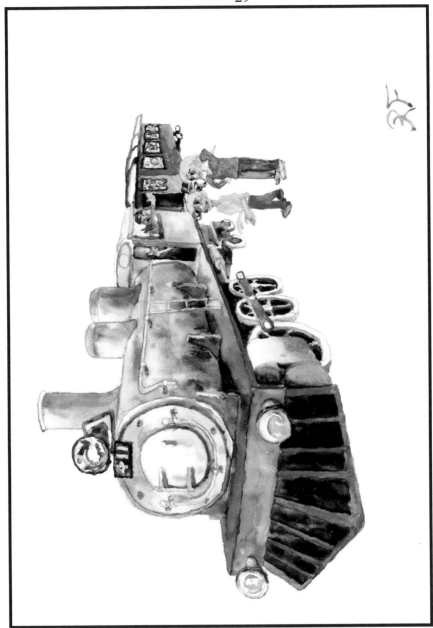

us to the front of the train where the conductor was. There were all sorts of levers and buttons; everything looked so neat and orderly.

Train Conductor: "Good morning Katie and Thomas! How is your Grandmother doing?"

Katie: "Wait. How do you know our names, and how do you know Grandma? We have never met you before."

Train Conductor: "You are mistaken Katie. I have been a good friend of your grandmother and grandfather for many years. I chose your grandfather as a gatekeeper to this world. After he died, your grandmother took over the job, and one day you and Thomas will be the new gate-keepers."

Thomas: "What kind of world is this?"

Train Conductor: "I am so glad you asked that question, Thomas. In fact, I already knew you were going to ask it before you asked the question. There are no boundaries to this world. There are no rules and there are no limits to what you can do. Let me prove it to you, Thomas. You can select anything in the animal kingdom, and experience what a day is like in its shoes. I can take you anywhere you want to go on Earth. Tell me Thomas, where have you always wanted to travel? Your wish is my command."

Thomas: "I want to travel to the ocean and see what it's like to be a tiger shark for the day!"

Katie: "You can't do that Thomas! It's underwater; the train can't go underwater, and we can't breathe underwater."

Train Conductor: "This is where you are wrong, Katie. In this world, anything is possible. There are no limitations, and there are no rules. Now run and grab a seat on the train and fasten your seat belts! This ride will get a little bumpy."

Thomas and I storm into the cabin directly behind the front of the train. The cabin has fancy red leather seats with gold-plated seatbelts. Thomas and I sit next to each other and strap ourselves in. As the train started, the cabin begins to vibrate and the train conductor blows the horn and yells "All ABOARD!" I wonder if there is anyone else on the train we haven't met. The woman in the black dress disappeared after she took us to meet the train conductor. The train finally started to move. We are traveling at about 30 miles per hour, and it feels like we are gaining more speed. The feeling is similar to taking off in an airplane. The train is still traveling in the cave, and I see light at the end where the cave ends. I think we are going 50 miles per hour now and the train is vibrating more and more as it picks up speed. We finally reached the end of the cave, and all of the sudden a huge light filled up our cabin followed by a loud bang. Thomas and I couldn't see anything because the light was so

bright. Instantly, the train stopped shaking and came to a
halt. It feels like we are floating. I looked out of the
window, and we are in the ocean. Thomas and I released
our seatbelts and ran to look out the window. The water
is clear and the ocean looked more beautiful then
anything I had ever seen. There are hundreds of exotic
fish with bright colors. I can see the bottom of the
ocean floor and to the right is a lot of coral reef with
bright colored plant life growing from it. Just then, an
intercom inside of the train turned on.

Train Conductor: "Will Thomas and Katie please come to
the front of the train. Your adventure awaits you."

Thomas and I raced to the front of the train. We didn't
know what to expect. Everything that was happening was
so unreal. We didn't understand how we got to the
bottom of the ocean, and we didn't understand how a
train could travel through water.

Train Conductor: "Welcome to the bottom of the Pacific
Ocean."

Katie: "How did we get to the bottom of the Pacific
Ocean so fast?"

Train Conductor: "When you have no limits to what you
can and cannot do, anything is possible. Now I want both
of you to put on these wet suits. We are going to meet a
good friend of mine. His name is Charles the Tiger Shark,

and he will show you what it is like to be a tiger shark. And remember, in this world you can breathe under water. The wet suits are for your protection so you do not get hurt."

I don't know how it is possible to breathe under water but considering everything else that has happened, I would not doubt it. This has been, by far, the most exciting day I have ever had, and our adventure is yet to begin. Thomas and I jumped into the water and it's true! We can breathe under water. I never thought anything like this was possible. The water is warm, too. Thomas and I spotted a shark coming toward the train. As it got closer, we could see the tiger stripes. That is when we knew it was Charles.

Charles: "Good afternoon Katie and Thomas! When I heard you would be traveling with me today I got excited. I know this is your first experience under water so you are in for quite a surprise!"

Charles is 10 feet long, 750 pounds, and 25 years old. He has beautiful tiger stripes all over his body, and he wears thick circular-shaped glasses. The glasses make him look like a very sophisticated tiger shark. Thomas seemed mesmerized by what was happening. I don't blame him; I was just as mesmerized as he was.

Thomas: "Are you going to take us on an adventure,

Charles?"

Charles: "Yes, Thomas. I am going to take you and Katie on an amazing adventure. We are currently in the Southern Pacific Ocean near Australia. Just like a regular tiger, I have few enemies, but that doesn't mean I don't have any. A life as a tiger shark is very stress free, and I do not have to worry about getting eaten, as long as I stay out of trouble. So let's get started on our adventure. I have not eaten anything all day, and I am very hungry. We are going to swim toward shallow water to search for food; now come follow me!"

Thomas and I began to follow Charles to shallow water in hopes of finding food. We spotted another tiger shark feeding on some larger fish he had caught. Charles decided to keep swimming because other tiger sharks do not like to share their food. As we swam further to shore, we spotted a dead fish floating in the water. Charles swam closer and took a bite out of the fish. Then we all spotted a great white shark that was much larger than Charles was. Charles realized the dead fish belonged to the great white shark and got us to swim away as fast as we could. A tiger shark has few enemies, but a great white is the king of the sea. Charles explained that he uses his nose to detect prey up to a quarter mile away. He smelled something very tasty so we swam to its location. It was a loggerhead sea turtle, and this was one of Charles's favorite treats. His teeth are sharp and powerful enough to bite right through the turtle's shell.

The sea turtle was bigger then me! Charles said that it was getting late, and we should travel back to the train. Along the way, we ran into a large school of fish, and Charles stopped to get a bite to eat. A couple other sharks his size noticed the school of fish so he swam away after a few tasty treats. Charles told us about the time he was in a feeding frenzy with other sharks and one of the sharks accidentally bit him trying to eat another fish. He said feeding frenzies are very dangerous, and you should avoid them at all costs. Charles likes to keep to himself as much as he can in order to stay alive. We finally reached the train, and it looked like our long adventure had ended. Thomas looked disappointed because he did not want the day to end.

Charles: "Thomas, I would like to ask you a few questions about today's adventure."

Thomas: "Sure Charles. You can ask me anything."

Charles: "Did you enjoy your adventure through the ocean?"

Thomas: "Of course I did; it was the greatest and most amazing adventure I have ever been on. I wish I could do it again and again and again."

Charles: "Then you realize how much fun it is to be a tiger shark. I have a wonderful life down here in the ocean. I can only imagine how much fun you would have if you were a tiger shark."

Thomas: "Being a tiger shark would be awesome!"

Charles: "What I am trying to say is we could trade places. I could be you, and you could be me as a tiger shark."

Katie: "Wait! Stop! You want to trade places with my brother? Will it be permanent?"

Charles: "Yes, Katie. Thomas can trade places with me and live a happy new life as a tiger shark. Remember Thomas, no one is here to tell you what to do; you have freedom down here. Back at home your mom and teachers tell you what to do."

Thomas: "You're right, Charles. I could do anything I want down here. I could swim anywhere without anyone telling me what to do. I could be free."

Katie: "No, Thomas. You need to stop and think about this. Remember the story that Grandmother told us, and the newspaper we found. The date was 1983; that is 26 years ago. Charles is 39 years old! He is the 13 year old boy from the newspaper!"

Thomas: "No he's not Katie. You don't know what you're talking about, and I have always wanted to be a tiger shark."

Katie: "No you haven't Thomas! The only reason you chose to go to the ocean and follow a tiger shark is because you saw the pictures on the wall in the cave. It wasn't even your own decision; you let the pictures decide for you."

Thomas: "No I didn't Katie. It is my decision, not yours!"

Thomas wakes up and he is excited as ever to explore the secret room. He notices that Katie is sound asleep. He jumps on her to wake her up.

Thomas: "Katie, wake up! It's time to explore the secret room, look how hard it is raining outside!"

Katie: "What are you talking about Thomas?! We already explored the secret room."

Thomas: "No we didn't Katie? We just woke up."

Thomas runs into the kitchen as Grandmother is making omelettes for all of us. Katie has a confused look on her face and is silent most of breakfast. Torn between a dream and reality, she does not know what to believe.

Grandmother: "Katie, hold your chin up"

Grandmother puts her hand right below Katie's chin and looks her right in the eye.

Grandmother: "I would stop thinking about why you know what you know and start thinking about how you are going to change what you know. Now are you two ready to explore the secret room?"

Thomas: "Yeah Grandma! I'm ready, I'm ready!"

Katie does not seem as excited as Thomas to explore the

secret room. She is still trying to put the pieces of what happened back together. Just then, Grandmother goes into her room to get the keys so they can open the door.

Katie: "Thomas, can you promise me one thing?"

Thomas: "Sure Katie, what is it?"

Katie: "What ever you do, you have got to promise me that you will not pick anything that has to do with Tiger Sharks."

Thomas: "What are you talking about Katie? I could not care less about tiger sharks."

Grandmother enters back into the room with the three keys. Thomas, Katie and Grandmother push the triangular shaped keys in all at once and turn to the right. The door opens and a boy is standing behind the door with a torch in his left hand to light up the cave. He is wearing thick circular shaped glasses. Katie and Thomas scream because they do not know who the boy is.

Grandmother: "Calm down children, I want you to meet a neighbor of mine. He is going to take you where you need to go. Don't get lost and remember to have fun!"

Grandmother went into the kitchen to get a match. She reached up to light the top right corner of the room, and suddenly, a huge flame appeared and continued to travel deep into the room. A medium sized path appeared. There are shelves about two feet below the ceiling. They look just like the shelves in the house that hold bonsai trees but instead of holding bonsai trees, they are holding a flame that lights up the entire pathway. Something feels all too familiar for Katie.

The End
Air all around me
There is a blue sky
After 26 years, I feel alive

I feel alive...

ABOUT THE AUTHOR

"The Mysterious Adventures of Cave Express" was two years in the making. I had always dreamed of owning my own book publishing service, but after graduating from the University of Baltimore with a major in Entrepreneurship Business Management, I decided to publish my own work instead. After completing the "Mysterious Adventures of Cave Express," I needed an artist to complete the work. A couple of months later, I ran into an old friend from high school, Robert Florio. When I found out how talented an artist he was, I asked him to illustrate the children's novel. Hesitant at first, I told him to read the book and get back to me. The next day I got a call from a very excited Rob, and he agreed to be the illustrator.

A lot of research and self-assessment went into the development of "The Mysterious Adventures of Cave Express." I wanted this to be a didactical work that drew upon my own experiences--experiences not of mystery and secrets but of learning, growing, and making informed choices. This is an adventure book that allows children to have insight into why they make certain decisions. As a child, I willfully made decisions without fully understanding why I made them. The inability to thoroughly assess the consequences of certain situations carried over to my schoolwork. As a result, my grades suffered. This book utilizes a climatic ending to stimulate the part of the brain used for reasoning. After reading this book, a child may be more inclined to view beyond the immediate situation and understand how a simple decision can affect the future.

THE ILLUSTRATOR
Robert Florio

Contact Information

Steven A. Jestes. Author,
    sajestes@gmail.com

Robert Florio. Illustrator,
    www.RobertFlorio.com

4578871

Made in the USA
Charleston, SC
12 February 2010